Dedicat

This book is dedicated to every BROWN girl needing to understand that they can heal the "little girl" within that struggles with low self-esteem, doesn't love herself, and unable to affirm herself.

Also, to every reader that finds a piece of themselves within the pages of this book. May you find strength and healing in my words!

I would like to thank Dr. Rashawana Smith, Denise Kelley, and the Higher Ground Mentees the push, encouragement, grace, and support to help bring this book to fruition! I love you all!!!!!

I love my pretty brown skin. My skin is radiant and perfect just the way it is. It is one of many brilliant

I am resilient. I am strong. I will always do my best. I am enough.

I am original, unique, and special. I am valuable, gifted, and creative. I accept and love myself as I am.

I am worthy. I am beautiful inside and out. My smile lights every room I'm in. I have a long rich heritage. My voice has power.

I am nerdy and confident. I am a leader and make good choices. I believe in myself. I am a strong, capable student.

I am a magnet for blessings. Blessings are overflowing everyday into my life. Because I am blessed, it is easy for me to bless others.

My voice matters.

I believe in myself. I can learn anything I put my mind to.

I have an unlimited potential within me.

I am kind. I treat others the way I want to be treated.

I am motivated. Difficult tasks are hard, but not impossible.

My body is beautifully perfect. It is perfect just for me. I am more than my shape or size! I am ALL things beautiful!

I am a pretty brown girl, so powerful and fearless! I attract happiness in my life! I am healthy, mind, body, and spirit! I am confident and successful! I am walking my own path!

Made in the USA
Monee, IL
15 September 2024